ABC
I Like Me!

by Nancy Carlson

PUFFIN BOOKS

This book is dedicated to the memory of my Grandma Dorothy. She was a *great* teller of jokes!

PUFFIN BOOKS
Published by the Penguin Group
Penguin Putnam Books for Young Readers, 345 Hudson Street, New York, New York 10014, U.S.A.
Penguin Books Ltd, 27 Wrights Lane, London W8 5TZ, England
Penguin Books Australia Ltd, Ringwood, Victoria, Australia
Penguin Books Canada Ltd, 10 Alcorn Avenue, Toronto, Ontario, Canada M4V 3B2
Penguin Books (N.Z.) Ltd, 182-190 Wairau Road, Auckland 10, New Zealand

Penguin Books Ltd, Registered Offices: Harmondsworth, Middlesex, England

First published in the United States of America by Viking, a division of Penguin Books USA Inc., 1997
Published by Puffin Books, a member of Penguin Putnam Books for Young Readers, 1999

40

THE LIBRARY OF CONGRESS HAS CATALOGED THE VIKING EDITION AS FOLLOWS:
Carlson, Nancy L.
ABC I like me! / Nancy Carlson.
p.   cm.
Summary: An alphabet book that explores self-esteem.
ISBN 0-670-87458-2 (hc.)
1. Self-esteem—Juvenile literature. 2. English language—Alphabet—Juvenile literature.
[1. Self-esteem. 2. Alphabet.] I. Title
BF697.5.S46C37 1997 158. 1—dc21 [E] 96-45118 CIP AC

Puffin Books ISBN 978-0-14-056485-3

Manufactured in Italy

Set in Publicity Gothic

**Feeling good about me
is as easy as ABC!**

I am Awesome,

Brave, and

Cheerful.

I have big Dreams,

and I like to Explore.

I am a good Friend.

I love to **Giggle**

and be Happy.

I have a great

Imagination.

I can **Jump** and **Juggle**.

I am **Kind**.

I am a good **L**eader.

Sometimes, I make Mistakes.

And sometimes, I'm Noisy!

I love to play **O**utside.

I try to be **Polite.**

I like **Q**uiet times

so I can Read.

I am good at **Sharing.**

I am Talented!

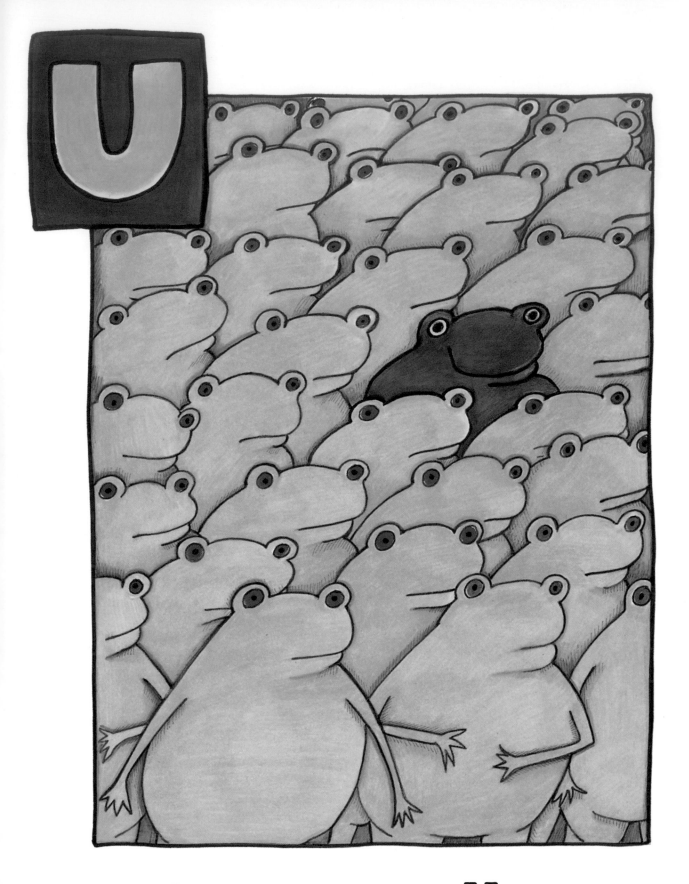

Look at me—I'm Unique!

I try to eat all my **V**egetables.

I like to make **Wishes**.

XXX ooo!

Yawn . . . I need a good

night's sleep, so tomorrow . . .

I can **Zoom** on!